THOM ROEP & PIET WIJN

Dusty Dabbert

The Secret Animal Kingdom

NOTHING IS BETTER THAN A WALK IN NATURE WHEN THE SUN IS SHINING. DUSTY IS SO HAPPY, HE STARTS SINGING.
ALONG FIELDS AND ***STREE-EEAMS,*** I WALK THROUGH THE ***TREE-EES...***

WHAT A PRETTY LITTLE BIRD. ARE YOU A ROBIN? WHAT DO YOU HAVE TO SAY?
TWEET!

YES, TWEET! YOUR USUAL REPORT.
COME HERE, LITTLE ONES, I HAVE SOME TREATS FOR YOU ALL.
RIBBIT!
RIBBIT!
TWEET!
2-1

TWEET!
TWEET!
IF ONLY I COULD UNDERSTAND YOU... JUST THINK HOW WONDERFUL IT WOULD BE TO TALK WITH YOU.
RIBBIT!

GOOD DAY, MADAM! LET ME HELP YOU WITH THAT HEAVY LOAD.

THAT'S VERY KIND OF YOU. I DON'T LIVE FAR AWAY.

SO WHAT BRINGS YOU TO OUR QUIET WOODS? ARE YOU LOOKING FOR SOMETHING?
I'M DUSTY DABBERT, AND I'M HERE BECAUSE I HAVEN'T BEEN HERE BEFORE.

HMMM...NOW THAT YOU'RE HERE, YOU BETTER LEAVE RIGHT AWAY, DUSTY. SOMETHING STRANGE IS GOING ON.

ONCE UPON A TIME, A LOT OF PEOPLE LIVED HERE, ESPECIALLY WOODCUTTERS. EVERYONE HAS LEFT NOW, EXCEPT FOR ME. I'M TOO OLD TO MOVE!
2-2

HERE WE ARE!
BUT WHY DID THEY ALL GO AWAY?

BECAUSE SOMETHING IS OFF! PEOPLE HEARD STRANGE VOICES IN THE MOUNTAINS OVER THERE. THEY WERE AFRAID OF GHOSTS!

WHERE DID THE VOICES COME FROM? WHOSE WERE THEY?
WHAT CAN I TELL YOU? YOU THINK PEOPLE WANTED TO LOOK CLOSER TO FIND OUT? POOH! THEY RAN AWAY LIKE RABBITS. AND NOW I'M HERE ALL BY MYSELF.
I HAVE TO ADMIT, I WOULDN'T WANT TO POKE MY NOSE IN EITHER. BETTER TO STAY AWAY FROM THOSE MOUNTAINS.

WELL, I'M CURIOUS ABOUT EXACTLY THAT KIND OF THING. I'LL POKE ***MY*** NOSE IN AND SEE WHAT'S GOING ON. THANK YOU FOR THE FRESH MILK!

WELL, I TRIED TO WARN HIM, SWEET PUSS. WE WON'T SEE ***HIM*** AGAIN...
2-3

DESPITE THE OLD WOMAN'S WARNING, DUSTY STARTS UP THE CLOSEST MOUNTAIN.
THAT WAS DEFINITELY NOT A CHEERY STORY, BUT CURIOSITY IS ONE OF MY WEAKNESSES...

AFTER ALL, I'VE SEEN A LOT OF THINGS IN MY LIFE, BUT NOT A GHOST, NOT YET. I CAN'T MISS THIS CHANCE.

A COUPLE OF HOURS LATER...
THIS MUST BE THE MOUNTAIN WHERE PEOPLE HEARD THE VOICES. I WONDER WHAT I'LL FIND.

IN FACT, THERE ARE CLEAR VOICES TO HEAR, BUT THERE'S NOTHING MYSTERIOUS ABOUT THEM. THEY COME FROM TWO RASCALS DUSTY HAS MET BEFORE.
PAY ATTENTION, YOU DOLT! YOU'LL BURN IT!
KLOINK!
IT'S ALMOST READY, SIR. OWWW!

WHAT? HOW DARE YOU GIVE ME THIS GARBAGE?
BUT SIR, YOU KNOW THAT'S THE LAST OF OUR SUPPLIES...
2-4

ARE WE STAYING HERE FOR A WHILE, SIR? IN THIS UNWELCOMING PLACE?
THEN I SUPPOSE I'LL HAVE TO EAT IT, THOUGH IT'S HARDLY THE ROYAL FEAST I'M USED TO.

OBVIOUSLY NOT, IDIOT. TOMORROW WE'LL CONTINUE OUR JOURNEY. IT'S BAD ENOUGH WE HAVE TO SPEND THE NIGHT IN THESE MISERABLE WOODS WITHOUT A SINGLE INN FOR TRAVELERS.

SO YOU'D BETTER START BUILDING A HUT FOR ME NOW, FOOL. IT DOESN'T HAVE TO BE BIG SINCE YOU'LL SLEEP OUTSIDE.
LISTEN, SIR, SOMEONE'S COMING!
INDEED! I HEAR SOMEONE WHISTLING. IF HE'S ALONE, YOU'LL JUMP HIM AND TAKE WHATEVER MONEY AND FOOD HE HAS.
ME, SIR? I HAVE TO DO THAT?

YES, YOU! AH, EXCELLENT, HE'S ALONE AND HE'S SMALL, TOO. GO GET HIM, DUMMY!
BUT...BUT...WE KNOW HIM! HE'S THE FUNNY FELLOW WHO WARNED THE KING NOT TO HIRE YOU AS THE PRINCESS' TUTOR.

YOU'RE RIGHT -- IT'S DUSTY, THAT STUPID BUSYBODY, ALWAYS POKING HIS NOSE WHERE IT DOESN'T BELONG!
JUST ANOTHER REASON TO ATTACK HIM -- NOW!
2-5

ZWIEP
?
HEY, WHAT'S GOING ON? LET ME GO!
CARL CRAVEN! HOW IS IT POSSIBLE?
IT'S A SMALL WORLD, ISN'T IT? I HAVE A BONE TO PICK WITH YOU, DUSTY! LOOK INSIDE HIS KNAPSACK, NINCOMPOOP!
WITH PLEASURE, SIR!
WHAOW!
CAN'T YOU DO ANYTHING RIGHT? OF ALL THE THINGS TO PULL OUT!
HAHAH HAHA! SERVES YOU RIGHT!
THE BAG IS EMPTY, SIR, EXCEPT FOR THE MOUSETRAP AND THIS BOOK.
?!
WHAT?
HONESTY IS THE BEST POLICY?
BAH!
EERLIJK DUURT HET LANGST
YOU'RE NOT EVEN WORTH ROBBING, YOU MISERABLE DWARF!
NITWIT, THROW HIM OFF THE CLIFF!
2-6

DUSTY IS IN A TIGHT SPOT!
?
WAIT, MORON! ON SECOND THOUGHT, HE MIGHT NOT BE COMPLETELY WORTHLESS. I HAVE A BETTER IDEA.

WHAT ARE YOU GOING TO DO, SIR?

WHAT DO YOU THINK, IMBECILE? WE'LL HOLD HIM FOR RANSOM. HE HAS GOOD FRIENDS AT COURT, REMEMBER? THEY SHOULD PAY AT LEAST HALF A MILLION GOLD COINS FOR HIM.
?
HAHAH HAHA!

WHAT'S SO FUNNY? WHAT DO YOU HAVE TO LAUGH ABOUT?
WHY NOT ASK FOR A FULL MILLION? I'M GETTING MORE VALUABLE BY THE MINUTE!
HE HAS A POINT, SIR. THE KING WASN'T SO KEEN ON HIM, EITHER.

WHO ASKED YOU, DUNDERHEAD?
LEAVE THE THINKING TO ME!
KLOINK
HAHAH HAHA!
2-7

TAKE THIS USELESS DWARF AWAY! GET HIM OUT OF MY SIGHT!
OEF!

NOW, DUNCE!
OKAY, CALM DOWN, I'LL TAKE CARE OF IT!

HEY, LOOK AT THAT! A DWARF-SIZED HOLE!

WAIT! STOP!

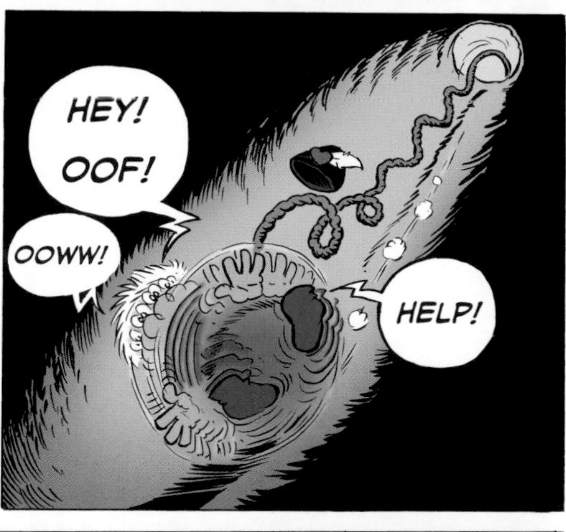
HEY! OOF!
OOWW!
HELP!

OOF!
WHAT NOW?
2-8

THERE, THAT'S THAT. THE CAVE IS DEEPER THAN I THOUGHT...HE FELL AT LEAST 20 FEET.

THAT TAKES CARE OF HIM FOR NOW. WE CAN PULL HIM UP TOMORROW MORNING AND GET OUT OF THIS PLACE. MAKE SURE THE HORSES ARE TIED UP AND GO TO SLEEP.
SLEEP WELL, SIR!

LATER...
WAKE UP, SIR! I HEAR VOICES COMING FROM THE CAVE.
WHAT?

IT'S THE BLASTED DWARF, OBVIOUSLY! TAKE YOUR BAG AND SHUT UP!

SEE, THAT WILL TEACH HIM. NOW GO TO SLEEP AND DON'T WAKE ME UNLESS IT'S IMPORTANT.

OW! FROM THE FEEL OF IT, THAT'S MY KNAPSACK.
BUT WHAT ABOUT THE VOICES?

HEY, WHAT'S THAT SOUND? IS SOMEONE COMING?
2-9

IS DUSTY IMAGINING THINGS?
I HEAR FOOTSTEPS ...AND I SEE LIGHT! SOMEONE IS DEFINITELY COMING!
HEY, ANYBODY? HELP ME! UNTIE ME!
CALM DOWN, I'M COMING. WHAT ARE YOU DOING HERE ANYWAY? YOU MUST KNOW THE CAVES OF ZOR ARE DANGEROUS.

WHAT?! AM I DREAMING? THIS CAN'T BE!
?!

BUT YOU AREN'T ONE OF US...WHAT KIND OF ANIMAL ARE YOU?
I'M A HUMAN.

NEVER HEARD OF IT, BUT I'LL GET YOU OUT OF THIS MESS.
I THOUGHT I'D SEEN A LOT, BUT HOW IS THIS POSSIBLE? A TALKING CAT?

HOW DID YOU LEARN HUMAN LANGUAGE?
IS THERE ANOTHER LANGUAGE WE SHOULD SPEAK?
ANYWAY, YOU'RE SPEAKING OUR LANGUAGE, SO IT'S ANIMAL LANGUAGE, NOT HUMAN, GET IT?

HMM, MAKES SENSE. ANYWAY, THANK YOU FOR THE HELP. I'M DUSTY DABBERT.
I'M PIF, THE GENERAL OF BAM.
2-10

WHAT IS BAM?
BAM IS OUR KING. BUT I'LL EXPLAIN EVERYTHING ON THE WAY. COME ALONG NOW...

WHERE?
TO THE VALLEY OF BAM, OF COURSE. OR WOULD YOU RATHER STAY IN THE DARK, DANK CAVES OF ZOR?

NO, DEFINITELY NOT! I'M VERY CURIOUS TO SEE YOUR WORLD AND MEET THIS BAM. I JUST NEED TO PREPARE A SURPRISE FOR MY TWO FRIENDS OUTSIDE.
?

AND SO DUSTY DISCOVERS THE MYSTERIOUS WORLD INSIDE THE MOUNTAIN.
HOW MANY OF YOU LIVE INSIDE THE MOUNTAIN?
WE NUMBER A FEW HUNDRED, BUT I DON'T KNOW WHAT MOUNTAIN YOU'RE TALKING ABOUT. WE LIVE IN THE VALLEY AND THIS IS THE FIRST TIME I'VE HEARD THAT OTHER PLACES EXIST BESIDES BAM'S VALLEY AND THE CAVES OF ZOR. NOBODY WILL BELIEVE IT!
2-11

HERE WE ARE, AT THE LAKE. WE JUST NEED TO CROSS IT AND WE'LL BE AT THE VALLEY.

WE'LL BE THERE SOON!

HOLD TIGHT, DUSTY. THE CURRENT IS STRONG HERE.

THROW THE TORCH IN THE WATER AND HOLD ON...WE'LL BE IN DAYLIGHT SOON.

WELCOME TO THE VALLEY OF BAM!
2-12

SO THIS IS THE VALLEY OF BAM! DUSTY STARES, ASTONISHED.
THIS IS UNBELIEVABLE! TALKING ANIMALS WEARING CLOTHES!
NOW I UNDERSTAND WHERE THE VOICES WERE COMING FROM THAT PEOPLE HEARD FROM OUTSIDE.
I DON'T KNOW WHAT YOU MEAN, DUSTY. WHAT IS "OUTSIDE"? TELL ME ABOUT YOUR WORLD.
I win!

SO DUSTY DOES...
WELL, SO THAT'S WHEN I DECIDED TO FIND OUT MORE ABOUT THE MYSTERIOUS VOICES...
GREETINGS, GENERAL! GREETINGS, STRANGER!

LIEUTENANT TORM REPORTING, SIR!

AAAGH!
A WILD BEAR! SAVE YOURSELF!

YOU DON'T HAVE TO BE AFRAID, DUSTY, LIEUTENANT TORM IS ONE OF MY OFFICERS.
?
SO HE'S NOT GOING TO EAT US?

HAHAHA! EAT YOU? WHAT AN IDEA! I WOULDN'T HURT A FLY!
2·13

IN THE VALLEY OF BAM, NOBODY EATS ANYBODY ELSE. IT'S STRICTLY FORBIDDEN. WE'RE FRIENDS TO EACH OTHER, NOT ENEMIES.

LIVE AND LET LIVE? ARE YOU SAYING EVERYONE LIVES IN PEACE HERE?
ABSOLUTELY! THAT'S NOT TRUE IN YOUR WORLD? DO HUMANS CAUSE TROUBLE?

AND HOW! IT'S PRACTICALLY ALL THEY DO!

WELL, THAT SOUNDS LIKE A SILLY KIND OF WORLD! WE'LL HEAR MORE ABOUT IT TOMORROW -- YOU NEED TO REST NOW. THE MOON IS OUT!
REST? THE DAY IS JUST STARTING WHERE I COME FROM.
COME STAY WITH ME, DUSTY.

HERE WE ARE, HOME SWEET HOME!
GOOD NIGHT, GENERAL! SWEET DREAMS, DUSTY!

A VALLEY WHERE TALKING ANIMALS LIVE IN PEACE.
I'VE STUMBLED INTO A WONDERFUL WORLD!
2-14

MEANWHILE...
WAKE UP, SIR, IT'S TIME.
YAWN!
YES, LET'S GO. PULL UP THE STUPID DWARF NOW.

HE'S NOT MOVING...HE'S STUCK SOMEHOW.
YOU'RE NOT STRONG ENOUGH BY YOURSELF, EH? I'LL GIVE YOU A HAND.

UGH!
HE'S VERY HEAVY FOR ONE SO SMALL!

OWW!
???

WHAT'S GOING ON HERE? THAT DWARF ESCAPED!
OOW! OOF!

HMM, SOMETHING STRANGE IS GOING ON. HE COULDN'T UNTIE HIMSELF NOW, COULD HE?
OOF! UGH!

HURRY UP, FOOL! YOU'RE GOING DOWN AND I'LL FOLLOW YOU.
BUT IT'S NOT SAFE...

SAFE OR NOT...
I CAN'T SEE A THING!
MOVE! I WANT TO SEE WHAT'S GOING ON.
2-15

THE NEWS OF DUSTY'S ARRIVAL SPREADS QUICKLY THROUGH THE VALLEY.
IT'S UNBELIEVABLE! NEVER HEARD OF SUCH A THING!
HE'S SOME SORT OF UNDISCOVERED **CREATURE!**
HE CALLS HIMSELF *HUMAN.*
HUMAN? WHAT'S THAT?

AT 11:00, BAM WILL MEET THIS STRANGER. WE ALL SHOULD BE THERE!
TORM SAYS HE'S A FRIENDLY, JOLLY FELLOW.

GREAT BAM, IT'S A PLEASURE FOR ME TO INTRODUCE YOU TO MY FRIEND, DUSTY DABBERT.
2-16

THANKS TO DUSTY'S MAGIC KNAPSACK, WHICH ALWAYS HAS WHATEVER HE NEEDS IN IT, DUSTY CAN OFFER A LOT OF GIFTS TO THE KING.
ALL FOR ME? THIS IS MOST GENEROUS OF YOU!
NOW TO THE TABLE. PLEASE SIT NEXT TO ME FOR OUR WELCOME FEAST.
WITH PLEASURE!
ALL THE FOOD IS DELICIOUS! NOW TELL ME ABOUT YOUR STRANGE WORLD.
AND SO DUSTY DOES...
SO CARL CRAVEN TOLD HIS SERVANT TO TIE ME UP AND THROW ME DOWN THE CAVE...
TERRIBLE! LET'S HOPE SUCH BAD BEHAVIOR NEVER COMES TO OUR VALLEY!
THOSE RASCALS WON'T FOLLOW ME. THEY'RE TOO COWARDLY TO DARE. I'M SURE THEY'RE MILES AWAY BY NOW.
GOSH DARNIT!
BLUB
BUT DUSTY IS WRONG ABOUT THIS...
2-17

WE WOULD BE HONORED IF YOU WOULD STAY WITH US A WHILE, DUSTY.
I'D LOVE TO, BAM. YOU'RE VERY KIND!
YOU'LL BE MY GUEST, OF COURSE, DUSTY. STAY WITH ME.
AND YOU MUST HAVE DINNER AT MY HOUSE.
I'D LOVE FOR YOU TO VISIT ME AS WELL!

WE NEED TO LEARN MORE ABOUT DUSTY'S WORLD, SO WE CAN GUARD AGAINST THE MEAN CREATURES HE'S DESCRIBED.
EXACTLY! WE NEED TO PROTECT OUR VALLEY FROM THEM!

WHERE ARE WE, SIR? IT LOOKS STRANGE.
?

IT LOOKS PERFECTLY ORDINARY. AND THERE'S AN INN!
2-18

DWARVES MUST LIVE HERE -- SEE HOW LOW THE CEILING IS!
HALLO!
ANYONE?
IT'S NOT LONG BEFORE CARL AND HIS SERVANT REACH THE INN.
I DON'T THINK ANYONE'S HERE NOW, SIR.
IT'S SO RUDE FOR AN INNKEEPER TO KEEP A NOBLEMAN LIKE MYSELF WAITING!
YOU'LL HAVE TO COOK FOR ME, DOLT!
AND HURRY UP!
YES, YES, I'M GOING!
SOON...
ISN'T IT ODD THAT NOBODY IS HERE? ANYWAY, I'M FIXING YOU A REAL FEAST. I FOUND A JUICY CHICKEN, THE BIGGEST YOU'VE EVER SEEN.
IMAGINE, THERE WASN'T ANY MEAT IN THE KITCHEN. THEN THIS CHICKEN WANDERED IN, LIKE A PET. IT WAS EVEN WEARING A LITTLE JACKET.
ANYWAY, IT'LL BE DELICIOUS!
A CHICKEN IN CLOTHES? HUH?
2-19

MEANWHILE...
WE ALWAYS MISS THE FUN. EVERYONE ELSE IS AT THE FEAST AND WE'RE STUCK ON PATROL.
WHAT DO YOU EXPECT? WE'RE SOLDIERS, NOT OFFICERS.

EVEN IF WE'D BEEN THE ONES TO FIND THE STRANGER, THE GENERAL WOULD HAVE TAKEN ALL THE CREDIT. IT'S ALWAYS THE SAME FOR US POOR SOLDIERS. THEY GET THE CAKE, WE GET THE CRUMBS.
BAH!

ANYWAY, MY STOMACH IS GROWLING. LET'S GET A BITE AT THE INN.
WE'RE ON DUTY, REMEMBER?

WHAT'S THAT?
I'VE NEVER SMELLED ANYTHING SO DELICIOUS IN MY LIFE!

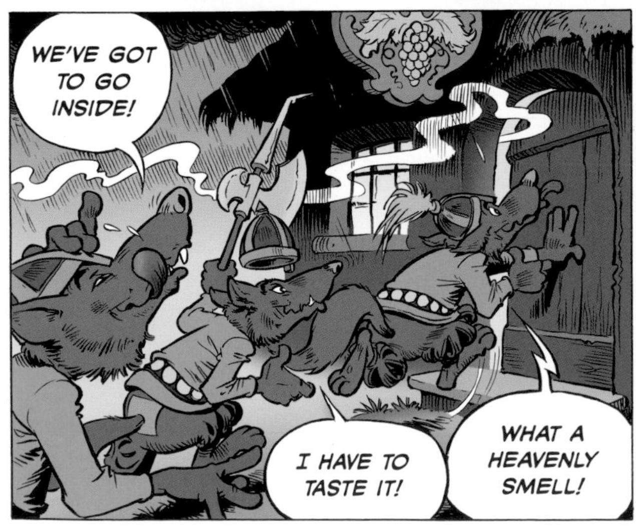
WE'VE GOT TO GO INSIDE!
I HAVE TO TASTE IT!
WHAT A HEAVENLY SMELL!

MORE HUMANS?
?
WOLVES!!!
AAAGH!!
2-20

CALM DOWN, HUMANS, WE WON'T HURT YOU.
WE'RE SORRY TO HAVE SCARED YOU. WE JUST WANT TO KNOW WHAT'S MAKING THAT SMELL.
FROM THIS... HAVE SOME...
YOU DON'T HAVE TO ASK TWICE!
YUMMM!
HOW IS IT POSSIBLE? TALKING ANIMALS?
MMMM GOOD!

I'M HAPPY TO MEET YOU. I'M CARL CRAVEN.
I'M ROF AND THIS IS KIL AND BOG. NOW TELL ME, WHAT IS THIS AMAZING DISH?
INNKEEPER! BRING SOME WINE FOR OUR FRIEND CARL!

NOBODY IS HERE, ROF. MY SERVANT COOKED THIS DISH HIMSELF.

THEN I'LL GET THE WINE.
BURP! THAT WAS DEEEELICIOUS! WHAT DID YOU SAY IT WAS?
IT WAS PERFECTLY ORDINARY...A ROASTED...

?
CHICKEN!!
WE'VE EATEN THE INNKEEPER! WE'RE MURDERERS!!

THE WOLVES GET OVER THEIR HORROR SOON ENOUGH...
THE INNKEEPER WAS A BIT OF A JERK ANYWAY, SO NO GREAT LOSS...
AND IT REALLY WAS AN INCREDIBLE DISH, THE BEST I'VE EVER EATEN.

BUT THINK ABOUT IT -- WE'LL BE BANNED! OR WORSE!
WE'RE CANNIBALS NOW AND IT'S ALL THEIR FAULT!

WHAT KIND OF FAULT? IN OUR WORLD, IT'S NATURAL FOR WOLVES TO EAT MEAT. EVERYONE DOES! AND YOU'VE TASTED YOURSELF HOW DELICIOUS IT IS.

HEH, HEH. I SEE SOME OPPORTUNITIES FOR US.
MORE WINE, DOLT!

YOU KNOW, CARL, I SEE MORE MEAT-EATING IN MY FUTURE.
HIC!

AND SO IT SHALL BE! FOLLOW ME AND I'LL GIVE YOU POWER, RICHES, AND MEAT EVERY DAY!
SOUNDS GOOD TO ME, HIC!
HIC!
2-22

GO OUT AND FIND ANOTHER CHICKEN OR SOME OTHER KIND OF MEAT -- QUICK!
BUT SIR, THE ANIMALS HERE TALK AND WEAR CLOTHES. THEY'RE LIKE PEOPLE...
SHUT UP AND DO WHAT I SAY, STUPID!
CARL'S PROMISES AND THE STRONG WINE HAVE THEIR EFFECT.
HIC!
WINE, MORE WINE! DOWN WITH BAM! LONG LIVE US -- AND CARL, OUR LEADER!
HIC!
HAHA HAHAHAH!
HEH, HEH, IT'S ALL GOING MY WAY! I'LL USE THESE FOOLS TO MAKE ALL THE ANIMALS HERE MY SLAVES. THEN I'LL SHOW THEM AROUND THE WORLD IN A CIRCUS! I'LL BE RICH, RICH, RICH!
I HOPE HE KNOWS WHAT HE'S DOING. I DON'T TRUST THOSE WOLVES! I'D RATHER GET OUT OF THIS STRANGE PLACE NOW!
2-23

HURRY UP OR WE'LL BE LATE TO THE BALL.
UH, OH! I FEEL SO MEAN -- THEY'RE TOO CUTE.
I JUST HAVE TO...
AND SO...
HELP!!
AH, HERE HE IS WITH SOME TASTY FOOD!
TAKE THEM TO THE KITCHEN AND GET TO WORK!
HAH, WE'LL HAVE A FEAST!
OOPS!
OH, NO! ONE ESCAPED, SIR!
YOU BUMBLING IDIOT! NOW HE'LL WARN EVERYONE ELSE!
2-24

WHILE HORRIBLE THINGS ARE HAPPENING AT THE INN, THE BALL IN DUSTY'S HONOR IS IN FULL SWING...
DUSTY IS SUCH A GOOD DANCER! HE'S CHARMING!
YOU HAVE A CRUSH!
HOORAY FOR DUSTY! HOORAY!
YOUR TAIL!
OH, NO!
HUH?
WHAT?
OOPS!
2·25

BONK!

IF THIS IS HOW HUMANS DANCE, IT'S A DANGEROUS BUSINESS. I'D CALL THIS MORE FALLING THAN DANCING.

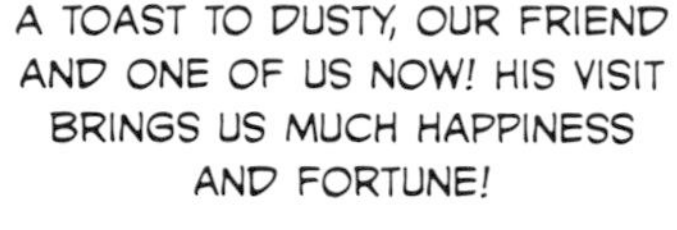
A TOAST TO DUSTY, OUR FRIEND AND ONE OF US NOW! HIS VISIT BRINGS US MUCH HAPPINESS AND FORTUNE!

CHEERS TO THAT!

HELP! DISASTER IS UPON US!

YOUR SOLDIERS, SIRE, THE WOLF PATROL, HAVE REBELLED! THEY'VE MURDERED AND EATEN THE INNKEEPER -- AND MY WIFE!
UH, OH...
WHAT?!

THEY GRABBED ME, TOO, BUT I GOT AWAY. THEY'RE BEING LED BY AN EVIL CREATURE...

?
?
!
SOMEONE LIKE HIM!
A HUMAN! EEEEEK!
2-26

STOP! DUSTY IS ONE OF US. HE'S NOT TO BLAME FOR THIS!
EVERYONE CALM DOWN AND STAY HERE. LIEUTENANT TORM WILL LEAD A PATROL TO SEE WHAT'S HAPPENING. WE NEED TO UNDERSTAND THIS NEW ENEMY.
SAY "AH!"
OUR LONGSTANDING PEACE WILL NOT BE BROKEN, I PROMISE YOU THAT!
LONG LIVE BAM, OUR KING!
WE TRUST YOU!
WE'LL BE BRAVE!
WE'RE TAKING NO RISKS, SOLDIERS. FOLLOW ME AND DO EXACTLY WHAT I SAY.
YES, SIR!

MEANWHILE THE WOLF PATROL HAS CONVINCED THE OTHER WOLVES TO JOIN THEM. IT WASN'T HARD...
LOOK AT THIS POWERFUL ARMY, ALL UNDER MY CONTROL, ALL FOR MY GLORY!
YES, SIR!
2-27

THE GENERAL AND HIS SOLDIERS ARE OFF TO FIND THE WOLVES.
FROM THE TOP OF THAT HILL, WE'LL HAVE A GOOD VIEW OF THE ENTIRE VALLEY.
CAREFUL, WE DON'T WANT TO BE SEEN OURSELVES.

OH, NO, THIS LOOKS BAD, VERY BAD.
HEY, THAT'S ROF!
AND KIL AND BOG, THE TRAITORS!
LET ME AT THOSE TURNCOATS!
CALM DOWN, WE'LL GET OUR CHANCE.

?
I WOULDN'T BE TOO SURE ABOUT THAT. DON'T MOVE OR YOU'RE DONE FOR!

WELL, LOOK WHO'S HERE, SOME SPIES!
WELCOME, FELLOWS. I'M CARL CRAVEN, YOUR LORD AND MASTER.
BE CAREFUL, CARL. THE BEAR IS STRONG.

HEHHEH! NOBODY IS STRONGER THAN ME! YOU'LL SEE!

A PIECE OF MEAT, ANYONE?
YOU HEARTLESS KILLER! YOU VILLAIN!
AAGH!
2-28

ENOUGH JOKING AROUND. SHUT THEM ALL UP SAFELY. YOU STAY HERE!

I'M SENDING YOU BACK TO YOUR NICE LITTLE KING WITH THIS MESSAGE, SO LISTEN GOOD...

AN HOUR LATER...
WE ALL HAVE TO SURRENDER TO CARL AND ROF AS OUR ABSOLUTE LEADERS. WE'RE SUPPOSED TO BE THEIR SLAVES. ***AND THEY WANT US TO CHOOSE WHICH ONES OF US THEY GET TO EAT!***
AAAGH!
WHAT??
THE DEVILS!

QUIET, QUIET!
LISTEN, EVERYONE!

THIS IS AN EMERGENCY AND WE MUST REMAIN CALM.
WE HAVE TO DEFEND OURSELVES!
YES, BUT HOW?

I DON'T KNOW...YET.
WELL, I DO!

WE CAN'T STAY IN THE VALLEY. WE'RE EASY MARKS HERE, TOO EASY TO FIND.

THERE'S ONLY ONE SOLUTION: WE ALL HAVE TO GET TO THE CAVES OF ZOR RIGHT AWAY!
2-29

THE CAVES OF ZOR?
HE'S CRAZY!
AND LEAVE ALL OUR STUFF FOR THEM TO TAKE?
IN THOSE CREEPY, DARK CAVES?

DUSTY IS RIGHT! BETTER TO LOSE SOME THINGS THAN YOUR LIVES! WE'RE GOING TO THE CAVES NOW!

AN EXCELLENT IDEA, DUSTY! WE'RE LUCKY TO HAVE YOU HERE.
POOH! IF HE WEREN'T HERE, THOSE EVIL DEVILS WOULDN'T HAVE FOLLOWED HIM TO OUR VALLEY.

HMMM...

AN HOUR LATER, ALL THE ANIMALS HEAD FOR THE CAVES, TOWARDS AN UNCERTAIN FUTURE.
2-30

ALL THE ANIMALS OF THE VALLEY ARE REFUGEES NOW...

LET ME HELP YOU UP.

WE'RE HERE.
NOW WHAT?
THE MOST IMPORTANT THING IS NOT TO PANIC.

OH, YOUR MAJESTY, HOW LONG DO WE HAVE TO STAY IN THESE MISERABLE CAVES? I DON'T KNOW HOW LONG I CAN MANAGE ...SNIFFLE.

DON'T WORRY, WE WON'T BE HERE LONG.
NOW ALL OF YOU LISTEN TO ME!
2-31

WE NEED TO STAY HERE A WHILE YET, SO PLEASE STAY CALM AND HELP EACH OTHER IN WHATEVER WAY YOU CAN. WE'RE IN THIS TOGETHER AND TOGETHER WE'LL STAY STRONG.

YOU'RE BRAVE ANIMALS AND WE WON'T BE SLAVES TO ANYONE! WE WILL SURVIVE THIS!
HE'S RIGHT. WE NEED TO TAKE CARE OF THE CHILDREN, PUT THEM TO BED.

THE ANIMALS START ORGANIZING SUPPER AND PLACES TO SLEEP, TRYING TO GET COZY.
IS THERE ANYTHING WE CAN DO TO HELP THE PATROL? THEY'RE FACING WOLVES, AFTER ALL!

NOTHING, I'M AFRAID. THEY'RE TRAINED SOLDIERS AND KNOW HOW TO HANDLE THEMSELVES. ALL WE CAN DO IS WAIT.

I NEED TO SEND A MESSAGE TO THAT VILLAIN, CARL CRAVEN. WRITE THIS DOWN.
IN RESPONSE TO ALL OF YOUR DEMANDS...
I'LL BRING THE MESSAGE!

NO, IT'S BEST I GO SINCE I KNOW THE RASCAL. I'VE HAD TO DEAL WITH HIM BEFORE.
THANK YOU, DUSTY. I KNOW I CAN COUNT ON YOU.
2-32

I THINK WE'VE SPENT ENOUGH TIME EATING AND DRINKING. IT'S TIME FOR THE SERIOUS PART NOW.
MAKE SURE ALL THE WOLVES ARE READY FOR THE GREAT BATTLE IN TEN MINUTES.
SIR, YES SIR!
THE GREAT BATTLE?
WHAT? HOW? DO YOU HAVE A PLAN, SIR?
YOU IDIOT, I'VE ALREADY EXPLAINED EVERYTHING TO YOU. MY WOLF ARMY WILL TAKE ALL THE ANIMALS PRISONER AND WE'LL BRING THEM TO OUR WORLD TO SHOW THEM IN OUR NEW CIRCUS.
I'LL BE RICH! THIS TIME, I'LL GET EVERYTHING I'VE EVER PLOTTED FOR -- MONEY, POWER, AND MORE MONEY!
ATTACK!
VICTORY WILL BE OURS!
2-33

THE BATTLE SIGNAL IS GIVEN.
ATTACK! TAKE EVERYONE PRISONER! WE'LL SAVE THE JUICIEST TO EAT!

HUH?
?
?
?

WHERE DID EVERYONE GO?
THEY'VE VANISHED!

YOU WORTHLESS FOOLS! WHERE ARE MY SLAVES? BURN THE PLACE DOWN!

WHAT'S THE POINT IN THAT, CARL? YOU'VE ALREADY LOST.

LOST?!
YOU! HOW DARE YOU?!
2-34

I'LL SHOW YOU!
NOW, NOW, A BIT OF CALM, PLEASE. I'M HERE TO NEGOTIATE. BY THE RULES OF WAR, YOU NEED TO LISTEN TO ME.
KING BAM WRITES, "IN RESPONSE TO ALL YOUR DEMANDS, WE SEND BACK AN ABSOLUTE REFUSAL TO YOUR EVIL PLAN...
ENOUGH!
TAKE HIM PRISONER!
TO TURN US INTO SLAVES OR MEAT. WE OFFER YOU A CHANCE TO LEAVE THE VALLEY IN PEACE..."
COWARD! I COME WITH THE WHITE FLAG! YOU HAVE TO... MUMMPH...
TO THE CAVES OF ZOR! THAT'S WHERE THEY MUST BE HIDING!

IN THE CAVES...
I'M WONDERING IF IT WAS A GOOD IDEA TO SEND DUSTY...
DUSTY IS CLEVER. HE'LL FIGURE SOMETHING OUT.

LOOK, LOOK, THEY'RE COMING!
2-35

OH, NO!
YOU'VE LIVED UP TO YOUR NAME, CRAVEN, TO TREAT A MESSENGER LIKE THAT.
AND YOU, ROF, HOW CAN YOU BE SUCH A *TRAITOR?*
THEY'VE GOT DUSTY!
SHUT UP! FOR SOMEONE WHO'S ABOUT TO DIE, YOU'RE VERY CHATTY. THE WOLVES OBEY *ME* NOW, NOT YOU!
YES! MEAT, WE WANT MEAT!

WHAT MEAT WILL YOU GIVE THEM? YOURSELVES? WE'VE SEALED EVERY ENTRANCE TO THE CAVES.

THERE'S ALWAYS THESE DELICIOUS HOSTAGES!

THAT'S NOT ENOUGH TO FEED AN ENTIRE WOLF ARMY. AND OUR SOLDIERS WOULD PROUDLY SACRIFICE THEMSELVES FOR US!
DON'T LISTEN TO HIS EMPTY PROMISES, WOLVES! THROW DOWN YOUR WEAPONS AND WE'LL FORGIVE YOU YOUR CRIMES!
WHAT NOW, CARL?
SIGH...

NEVER!
ATTACK! FIND A WAY IN!

WE'LL GET YOU ALL! HEHHEHEH!
2-36

EVERYTHING IS READY TO KEEP OUT THE WOLVES.
SEAL EVERY CRACK! WE'RE SAFE FOR NOW!

IS EVERYTHING SHUT TIGHT?
YES, SIRE. ALL EXCEPT SOME CRACKS OVERHEAD. I DOUBT THEY CAN GET THROUGH THERE.

NO, IT LOOKS TOO NARROW.

HMMPH! IF I HAD SOME GUNPOWDER -- OR EXPLOSIVES!
IT'S IMPOSSIBLE, MR. CARL. THEY'VE BLOCKED EVERY HOLE. THERE'S NO WAY IN.

HERE, HERE! I FOUND SOMETHING!
YOU? THE FOOL?

COME THIS WAY -- YOU CAN SEE THEM!
?

LOOK, WE'RE RIGHT OVER THEM. YOU CAN HEAR THEIR VOICES!
WELL, I'LL BE!
2-37

AND SO...
ALL WE HAVE TO DO IS TAKE AWAY THE SANDBAGS. THE WATER WILL DO THE WORK FOR US. IT'S PURE GENIUS!
SHOVE THE STUPID DWARF THROUGH FIRST, SO HE CAN LET HIS FRIENDS KNOW THEIR HORRIBLE FATE.
DUSTY! IT'S DUSTY!
THEY'RE LETTING HIM GO?
!
WHAT'S HAPPENING?
WHY DID THEY LET YOU GO?
HAHAHAHAHAH! DUSTY ISN'T THE ONLY PRESENT WE HAVE FOR YOU! JUST YOU WAIT!!
NOW!
ARE YOU COZY IN YOUR CAVES? NOT FOR LONG! I'LL SEE YOU OUTSIDE!
WE NEED TO GET OUT OR WE'LL DROWN!
2-38

FASTER, HIGHER, FASTER!
THIS WAY, EVERYONE!
FOLLOW ME!

MOVE THE BLOCKADE AND GET OUT AS FAST AS YOU CAN.
BLUB

SURRENDER TO THEM PEACEFULLY, BUT MAKE SURE YOU DON'T BLOCK THE TUNNEL ENTRANCE.
BUT DUSTY...

JUST GO, BAM. YOU HAVE TO TRUST ME.

GIVE ME A HAND, GENERAL.

WE HAVEN'T LOST YET. RUN DOWN TO THE VALLEY, BRINGING THE ROPE ALONG WITH YOU.
?
2-39

VILLAINS!
IT SEEMS CARL AND HIS WOLF ARMY HAVE WON AFTER ALL.
YUMM, FRESH EGGS!
WELCOME, TURTLE SOUP!

YOU SEE, MY WOLVES, I AM A GREAT, CLEVER LEADER! AND WHICH ONE OF THESE IDIOTS IS BAM?
HAHAHA!
HEH! WHO IS BAM, HOW FUNNY!

YOU HAVEN'T WON YET, COWARD!
?

WE WILL NEVER SURRENDER!
!
?

YOU DON'T *DARE* GRAB US!
THOSE JOKERS ARE BEGINNING TO BORE ME. GO GET THEM.
KILL 'EM!
2-40

NOW, PIF, NOW!
SPLASJ
WHAT THE...

NOW IT'S OUR TURN TO USE WATER!
EVERYONE, GET THE WOLVES!
BLUB

DROP YOUR WEAPONS, WOLVES! I HAVE YOUR LEADER!

I INSIST YOU ALL...
!
YOU INSIST NOTHING. THE SCORE IS ONE-ONE.
2-41

WHAT'S YOUR PLAN NOW, DWARF?
DON'T SURRENDER!
I DIE FOR MY ANIMALS!
NEVER! LET THE WOLF LEADER GO!
MERCY!
WE'RE EVEN, CARL! LET'S BOTH PUT DOWN OUR WEAPONS!
AGREED! THE FIGHT IS FINISHED. WE'LL DEAL WITH YOU LATER.
BOING
NO, THAT WON'T DO. YOU PROMISED THE WOLVES MEAT AND I PROMISED THE ANIMALS PEACE...
THAT MEANS BOTH PARTIES NEED TO GET SOMETHING. THERE WILL BE PEACE AND YOUR WOLVES CAN EAT MEAT.
WHAT?!
TRAITOR!
YOU'RE CRAZY!
DUSTY, HOW COULD YOU!
CALM DOWN!
WE CAN'T TRUST HIM!
?
I KNOW WHAT I'M DOING! I'LL TEACH THEM A LESSON ALRIGHT...
2-42

THE DECISION IS MADE TO DRAW LOTS TO SEE WHO GETS EATEN.
DUSTY, WHAT ARE YOU DOING!?
TRAITOR! YOU'RE OFFERING US UP TO KILLERS!
A LITTLE CALM, PLEASE! I JUST NEED MY KNAPSACK BACK.

IS EVERYONE'S NAME ON A SLIP OF PAPER? THEN PUT THEM IN!

DUSTY, YOU CAN'T...
TRUST ME, BAM.
GENERAL PIF, DID YOU WRITE EVERYONE'S NAME DOWN?
YES, AND THE WOLVES HAVE CHECKED THEM ALL.
WE HAVE!

THEN YOU GET TO DECIDE WHO WILL LIVE IN PEACE, AND WHO WILL BE EATEN...
NOT ME!

ENOUGH! I'M NOT AFRAID TO PICK!

THE FIRST TO BE EATEN IS...
2·43

ROF, THE WOLF!
THIS CAN'T HAPPEN! IT'S WRONG!
YOU PICKED! YOU'RE THE ONE TO BLAME!
BUT WE THOUGHT... I MEAN...
THAT YOU COULDN'T BE MEAT? BUT YOU CAN!
WHAT A TERRIBLE IDEA, TO EAT EACH OTHER!
CAN'T WE LIVE IN PEACE, LIKE BEFORE?
HELP! DON'T HIT!
YOU STARTED ALL THIS!
FORGIVE US, SIRE, HAVE MERCY!
THAT WAS BEFORE THESE TWO RASCALS GOT HERE!
EXACTLY! IT'S THEIR FAULT ALL THIS HAPPENED!
WE'LL NEVER EAT MEAT AGAIN!
SMOOCH
2.44

AND SO ALL THE ANIMALS RETURN HOME IN PEACE.

EXPLAIN TO ME HOW YOU COULD TAKE SUCH A RISK, DUSTY?
IT WASN'T A RISK AT ALL!

LOOK!
WHAT? EACH PAPER SAYS 'WOLF'!
WOLF

BUT I WROTE THE NAMES DOWN MYSELF. WE WERE ALL THERE...
YES, BUT THEN YOU PUT THEM IN MY MAGIC KNAPSACK -- AND IT ALWAYS HAS EXACTLY WHAT I NEED!

MEANWHILE...
HURRY UP, FOOL, WE'VE GOT TO GET OUT OF HERE NOW!
2-45

AND SO EVERYTHING ENDS HAPPILY EVER AFTER.
DON'T YOU WANT TO STAY WITH US, DUSTY?
I'M TEMPTED, BAM, BUT THERE ARE TOO MANY THINGS I HAVEN'T SEEN YET -- INCLUDING GHOSTS. TOMORROW I'LL BE OFF.
HOORAY FOR DUSTY!
OUR HERO!
YOUR KINGDOM CAN BE A SECRET ONCE AGAIN. THOSE TWO RASCALS WON'T WANT ANYONE TO KNOW ABOUT THEIR FAILURE HERE. BUT I'M GLAD TO KNOW WHERE YOU ARE -- AND I HOPE TO VISIT AGAIN ONE DAY.
THE END